THE GETTY
AND OTHER SPEECHES

ABRAHAM LINCOLN

THE GETTYSBURG ADDRESS AND OTHER SPEECHES

penguin books

PENGUIN BOOKS
Published by the Penguin Group
Penguin Books USA Inc., 375 Hudson Street,
New York, New York 10014, U.S.A.
Penguin Books Ltd, 27 Wrights Lane,
London W8 5TZ, England
Penguin Books Australia Ltd, Ringwood,
Victoria, Australia
Penguin Books Canada Ltd, 10 Alcorn Avenue,
Toronto, Ontario, Canada M4V 3B2
Penguin Books (N.Z.) Ltd, 182–190 Wairau Road,
Auckland 10, New Zealand

Penguin Books Ltd, Registered Offices:
Harmondsworth, Middlesex, England

Published in Penguin Books 1995

ISBN 0 14 60.0079 X

Printed in the United States of America

CONTENTS

Announcement to the People
of Sangamo County, Illinois:
March 9, 1832

Fellow-Citizens:

Having become a candidate for the honorable office of one of your representatives in the next General Assembly of this state, in accordance with an established custom, and the principles of true republicanism, it becomes my duty to make known to you—the people whom I propose to represent—my sentiments with regard to local affairs.

Time and experience have verified to a demonstration, the public utility of internal improvements. That the poorest and most thinly populated countries would be greatly benefitted by the opening of good roads, and in the clearing of navigable streams within their limits, is what no person will deny. But yet it is folly to undertake works of this or any other kind, without first knowing that we are able to finish them—as half finished work generally proves to be labor lost. There cannot justly be any objection to having rail roads and canals, any more than to other good things, provided they cost nothing. The only objection is to paying for them; and the objection to paying arises from the want of ability to pay.

With respect to the County of Sangamo, some more easy

means of communication than we now possess, for the purpose of facilitating the task of exporting the surplus products of its fertile soil, and importing necessary articles from abroad, are indispensably necessary. A meeting has been held of the citizens of Jacksonville, and the adjacent country, for the purpose of deliberating and enquiring into the expediency of constructing a railroad from some eligible point on the Illinois river, through the town of Jacksonville, in Morgan county, to the town of Springfield, in Sangamo county. This is, indeed, a very desirable object. No other improvement that reason will justify us in hoping for, can equal in utility the rail road. It is a never failing source of communication, between places of business remotely situated from each other. Upon the rail road the regular progress of commercial intercourse is not interrupted by either high or low water, or freezing weather, which are the principal difficulties that render our future hopes of water communication precarious and uncertain. Yet, however desirable an object the construction of a rail road through our country may be; however high our imaginations may be heated at thoughts of it—there is always a heart appalling shock accompanying the account of its cost, which forces us to shrink from our pleasing anticipations. The probable cost of this contemplated rail road is estimated at $290,000;—the bare statement of which, in my opinion, is sufficient to justify the belief, that the improvement of the Sangamo river is an object much better

suited to our infant resources.

Respecting this view, I think I may say, without the fear of being contradicted, that its navigation may be rendered completely practicable, as high as the mouth of the South Fork, or probably higher, to vessels of from 25 to 30 tons burthen, for at least one half of all common years, and to vessels of much greater burthen a part of that time. From my peculiar circumstances, it is probable that for the last twelve months I have given as particular attention to the stage of the water in this river as any other person in the country. In the month of March, 1831, in company with others, I commenced the building of a flat boat on the Sangamo, and finished and took her out in the course of the spring. Since that time, I have been concerned in the mill at New Salem. These circumstances are sufficient evidence, that I have not been very inattentive to the stages of the water.——The time at which we crossed the mill dam, being in the last days of April, the water was lower than it had been since the breaking of winter in February, or than it was for several weeks after. The principal difficulties we encountered in descending the river, were from the drifted timber, which obstructions all know is not difficult to be removed. Knowing almost precisely the height of water at that time, I believe I am safe in saying that it has as often been higher as lower since.

From this view of the subject, it appears that my calculations with regard to the navigation of the Sangamo cannot be unfounded in reason; but whatever may be its 3 natural advantages, certain it is, that it never can be practically useful to any great extent, without being greatly improved by art. The drifted timber, as I have before mentioned, is the most formidable barrier to this object. Of all parts of this river, none will require so much labor in proportion, to make it navigable, as the last thirty or thirty-five miles; and going with the meanderings of the channel, when we are this distance above its mouth, we are only between twelve and eighteen miles above Beardstown, in something near a straight direction; and this route is upon such low ground as to retain water in many places during the season, and in all parts such as to draw two-thirds or three-fourths of the river water at all high stages.

This route is upon prairie land the whole distance;—so that it appears to me, by removing the turf, a sufficient width and damming up the old channel, the whole river in a short time would wash its way through, thereby curtailing the distance, and increasing the velocity of the current very considerably, while there would be no timber upon the banks to obstruct its navigation in future; and being nearly straight, the timber which might float in at the head, would be apt to go clear through. There are also many places above this where the river, in its zig zag course, forms such complete peninsulas, as to be easier

4 cut through at the necks than to remove the obstructions

from the bends—which, if done, would also lessen the distance.

What the cost of this work would be, I am unable to say. It is probable, however, it would not be greater than is common to streams of the same length. Finally, I believe the improvement of the Sangamo river, to be vastly important and highly desirable to the people of this county; and if elected, any measure in the legislature having this for its object, which may appear judicious, will meet my approbation, and shall receive my support.

It appears that the practice of loaning money at exorbitant rates of interest, has already been opened as a field for discussion; so I suppose I may enter upon it without claiming the honor, or risking the danger, which may await its first explorer. It seems as though we are never to have an end to this baneful and corroding system, acting almost as prejudicial to the general interests of the community as a direct tax of several thousand dollars annually laid on each county, for the benefit of a few individuals only, unless there be a law made setting a limit to the rates of usury. A law for this purpose, I am of opinion, may be made without materially injuring any class of people. In cases of extreme necessity there could always be means found to cheat the law, while in all other cases it would have its intended effect. I would not favor the passage of a law upon this subject, which might be very easily evaded. Let it be such that the labor and difficulty of evading it, could only be justified in cases of the greatest necessity.

Upon the subject of education, not presuming to dictate any plan or system respecting it, I can only say that I view it as the most important subject which we as a people can be engaged in. That every man may receive at least, a moderate education, and thereby be enabled to read the histories of his own and other countries, by which he may duly appreciate the value of our free institutions, appears to be an object of vital importance, even on this account alone, to say nothing of the advantages and satisfaction to be derived from all being able to read the scriptures and other works, both of a religious and moral nature, for themselves. For my part, I desire to see the time when education, and by its means, morality, sobriety, enterprise and industry, shall become much more general than at present, and should be gratified to have it in my power to contribute something to the advancement of any measure which might have a tendency to accelerate the happy period.

With regard to existing laws, some alterations are thought to be necessary. Many respectable men have suggested that our estray laws—the law respecting the issuing of executions, the road law, and some others, are deficient in their present form, and require alterations. But considering the great probability that the framers of those laws were wiser than myself, I should prefer [not?] meddling with them, unless they were first attacked by others, in which case I should feel it both a privilege and a duty to take that stand, which in my view, might tend most to the advancement of justice.

But, Fellow-Citizens, I shall conclude.—Considering the great degree of modesty which should always attend youth, it is probable I have already been more presuming than becomes me. However, upon the subjects of which I have treated, I have spoken as I thought. I may be wrong in regard to any or all of them; but holding it a sound maxim, that it is better to be only sometimes right, than at all times wrong, so soon as I discover my opinions to be erroneous, I shall be ready to renounce them.

Every man is said to have his peculiar ambition. Whether it be true or not, I can say for one that I have no other so great as that of being truly esteemed of my fellow men, by rendering myself worthy of their esteem. How far I shall succeed in gratifying this ambition, is yet to be developed. I am young and unknown to many of you. I was born and have ever remained in the most humble walks of life. I have no wealthy or popular relations to recommend me. My case is thrown exclusively upon the independent voters of this county, and if elected they will have conferred a favor upon me, for which I shall be unremitting in my labors to compensate. But if the good people in their wisdom shall see fit to keep me in the back

ground, I have been too familiar with disappointments to
be very much chagrined.

Your friend and fellow-citizen,

A. Lincoln

Notes on Lawyers:
ca. July 1, 1850

I am not an accomplished lawyer. I find quite as much material for a lecture in those points wherein I have failed, as in those wherein I have been moderately successful. The leading rule for the lawyer, as for the man of every other calling, is diligence. Leave nothing for tomorrow which can be done today. Never let your correspondence fall behind. Whatever piece of business you have in hand, before stopping, do all the labor pertaining to it which can then be done. When you bring a common law suit, if you have the facts for doing so, write the declaration at once. If a law point be involved, examine the books, and note the authority you rely on upon the declaration itself, where you are sure to find it when wanted. The same of defenses and pleas. In business not likely to be litigated,—ordinary collection cases, foreclosures, partitions, and the like,—make all examinations of titles, and note them, and even draft orders and decrees in advance. This course has a triple advantage; it avoids omissions and neglect, saves your labor when once done, performs the labor out of court when you have leisure, rather than in court when you have not. Extemporaneous speaking should be practiced and cultivated. It is the lawyer's avenue to the public. However able and faithful he may be in other respects, people are slow to bring him business if he cannot make a speech. And yet there is not a more fatal error to young lawyers than relying too much on speech-making. If anyone, upon his rare powers of speaking, shall claim an exemption from the drudgery of the law, his case is a failure in advance.

Discourage litigation. Persuade your neighbors to compromise whenever you can. Point out to them how the nominal winner is often a real loser—in fees, expenses, and waste of time. As a peacemaker the lawyer has a superior opportunity of being a good man. There will still be business enough.

Never stir up litigation. A worse man can scarcely be found than one who does this. Who can be more nearly a fiend than he who habitually overhauls the register of deeds in search of defects in titles, whereon to stir up strife, and put money in his pocket? A moral tone ought to be infused into the profession which should drive such men out of it.

The matter of fees is important, far beyond the mere question of bread and butter involved. Properly attended to, fuller justice is done to both lawyer and client. An exorbitant fee should never be claimed. As a general rule never take your whole fee in advance, nor any more than a small retainer. When fully paid beforehand, you are more than a common mortal if you can feel the same interest in the case, as if something was still in prospect for you, as well as for your client. And when you lack interest in the case the job will very likely lack skill and diligence in the performance. Settle the amount of fee and take a note in advance. Then you will feel that you are working for something, and you are sure to do your work faithfully and well. Never sell a fee note—at least not before the consideration service is performed. It leads to negligence and dishonesty—negligence by losing interest in the case, and dishonesty in refusing to refund when you have allowed the consideration to fail.

There is a vague popular belief that lawyers are necessarily dishonest. I say vague, because when we consider to what extent confidence and honors are reposed in and conferred upon lawyers by the people, it appears improbable that their impression of dishonesty is very distinct and vivid. Yet the impression is common, almost universal. Let no young man choosing the law for a calling for a moment yield to the popular belief—resolve to be honest at all events; and if in your own judgment you cannot be an honest lawyer, resolve to be honest without being a lawyer. Choose some other occupation, rather than one in the choosing of which you do, in advance, consent to be a knave.

A House Divided: Speech Delivered at Springfield, Illinois at the Close of the Republican State Convention: June 16, 1858

Mr. President and Gentlemen of the Convention:

If we could first know *where* we are, and *whither* we are tending, we could then better judge *what* to do, and *how* to do it.

We are now far into the *fifth* year, since a policy was initiated, with the *avowed* object, and *confident* promise, of putting an end to slavery agitation.

Under the operation of that policy, that agitation has not only, *not ceased,* but has *constantly augmented.*

In *my* opinion, it *will* not cease, until a *crisis* shall have been reached, and passed.

"A house divided against itself cannot stand."

I believe this government cannot endure, permanently half-*slave* and half-*free.*

I do not expect the Union to be *dissolved*—I do not expect the house to *fall*—but I *do* expect it will cease to be divided.

It will become *all* one thing, or *all* the other.

Either the *opponents* of slavery, will arrest the further spread of it, and place it where the public mind shall rest in the belief that it is in course of ultimate extinction; or its *advocates* will push it forward, till it shall become alike lawful in *all* the states, *old* as well as *new*—*North* as well as *South*.

Have we no *tendency* to the latter condition?

Let any one who doubts, carefully contemplate that now almost complete legal combination—piece of *machinery* so to speak—compounded of the Nebraska doctrine, and the Dred Scott decision. Let him consider not only *what work* the machinery is adapted to do, and *how well* adapted; but also, let him study the *history* of its construction, and trace, if he can, or rather *fail*, if he can, to trace the evidences of design, and concert of action, among its chief bosses, from the beginning.

But, so far, *Congress* only, had acted; and an *indorsement* by the people, *real* or apparent, was indispensable, to *save* the point already gained, and give chance for more.

The new year of 1854 found slavery excluded from more than half the states by state constitutions, and from most of the national territory by congressional prohibition.

Four days later, commenced the struggle, which ended in repealing that congressional prohibition.

This opened all the national territory to slavery; and was the first point gained.

This necessity had not been overlooked; but had been provided for, as well as might be, in the notable argument of *"squatter sovereignty,"* otherwise called *"sacred right of* 13 *self-government,"* which latter phrase, though expressive of the only rightful basis of any government, was so perverted in this attempted use of it as to amount to just this: That if any *one* man, choose to enslave *another*, no *third* man shall be allowed to object.

That argument was incorporated into the Nebraska bill itself, in the language which follows: *"It being the true intent and meaning of this act not to legislate slavery into any territory or state, nor exclude it therefrom; but to leave the people thereof perfectly free to form and regulate their domestic institutions in their own way, subject only to the Constitution of the United States."*

Then opened the roar of loose declamation in favor of "Squatter Sovereignty," and "sacred right of self-government."

"But," said opposition members, "let us be more *specific*—let us *amend* the bill so as to expressly declare that the people of the territory *may* exclude slavery." "Not we," said the friends of the measure; and down they voted the amendment.

While the Nebraska bill was passing through Congress, a *law case,* involving the question of a Negro's freedom, by reason of his owner having voluntarily taken him first into a free state and then a territory covered by the congressional prohibition, and held him as a slave, for a long time in each, was passing through the U. S. Circuit Court for the District of Missouri; and both Nebraska bill and law suit were brought to a decision in the same month of May, 1854. The Negro's name was "Dred Scott," which name now designates the decision finally made in the case.

Before the *then* next presidential election, the law case came *to*, and was argued *in* the Supreme Court of the United States; but the *decision* of it was deferred until *after* the election. Still, *before* the election, Senator Trumbull, on the floor of the Senate, requests the leading advocate of the Nebraska bill to state *his opinion* whether people of a territory can constitutionally exclude slavery from their limits; and the latter answers, "That is a question for the Supreme Court."

The election came. Mr. Buchanan was elected, and the *indorsement*, such as it was, secured. That was the *second* point gained. The indorsement, however, fell short of a clear popular majority by nearly four hundred thousand votes, and so, perhaps, was not overwhelmingly reliable and satisfactory.

The *outgoing* President, in his last annual message, as impressively as possible *echoed back* upon the people the *weight* and *authority* of the indorsement.

The Supreme Court met again; *did not* announce their decision, but ordered a re-argument.

The presidential inauguration came, and still no decision of the court; but the *incoming* President, in his inaugural address, fervently exhorted the people to abide by the forthcoming decision, *whatever it might be*.

Then, in a few days, came the decision.

The reputed author of the Nebraska bill finds an early occasion to make a speech at this capitol indorsing the Dred Scott decision, and vehemently denouncing all opposition to it.

The new President, too, seizes the early occasion of the Silliman letter to *indorse* and strongly *construe* that decision, and to express his *astonishment* that any different view had ever been entertained.

At length a squabble springs up between the President and the author of the Nebraska bill, on the *mere* question of *fact*, whether the Lecompton constitution was or was not, in any just sense, made by the people of Kansas; and in that squabble the latter declares that all he wants is a fair vote for the people, and that he *cares* not whether slavery be voted *down* or voted *up.* I do not understand his declaration that he cares not whether slavery be voted down or voted up, to be intended by him other than as an *apt definition* of the *policy* he would impress upon the public mind—the *principle* for which he declares he has suffered much, and is ready to suffer to the end.

And well may he cling to that principle. If he has any parental feeling, well may he cling to it. That principle, is the only *shred* left of his original Nebraska doctrine.

16 Under the Dred Scott decision, "squatter sovereignty"

squatted out of existence, tumbled down like temporary scaffolding—like the mould at the foundry served through one blast and fell back into loose sand—helped to carry an election, and then was kicked to the winds. His late *joint* struggle with the Republicans, against the Lecompton constitution, involves nothing of the original Nebraska doctrine. That struggle was made on a point, the right of a people to make their own constitution, upon which he and the Republicans have never differed.

The several points of the Dred Scott decision, in connection with Senator Douglas' "care not" policy, constitute the piece of machinery, in its *present* state of advancement. This was the third point gained.

The *working* points of that machinery are:

First, that no Negro slave, imported as such from Africa, and no descendant of such slave can ever be a *citizen* of any state, in the sense of that term as used in the Constitution of the United States.

This point is made in order to deprive the Negro, in every possible event, of the benefit of this provision of the United States Constitution, which declares that—

"The citizens of each state shall be entitled to all privileges and immunities of citizens in the several states."

Secondly, that "subject to the Constitution of the United States," neither *Congress* nor a *Territorial Legislature* can exclude slavery from any United States territory.

This point is made in order that individual men may

fill up the territories with slaves, without danger of losing them as property, and thus to enhance the chances of *permanency* to the institution through all the future.

Thirdly, that whether the holding a Negro in actual slavery in a free state, makes him free, as against the holder, the United States courts will not decide, but will leave to be decided by the courts of any slave state the Negro may be forced into by the master.

This point is made, not to be pressed *immediately;* but, if acquiesced in for a while, and apparently *indorsed* by the people at an election, *then* to sustain the logical conclusion that what Dred Scott's master might lawfully do with Dred Scott, in the free state of Illinois, every other master may lawfully do with any other *one*, or one *thousand* slaves, in Illinois, or in any other free state.

Auxiliary to all this, and working hand in hand with it, the Nebraska doctrine, or what is left of it, is to *educate* and *mould* public opinion, at least *Northern* public opinion, to not *care* whether slavery is voted *down* or voted *up*.

This shows exactly where we now *are;* and *partially* also whither we are tending.

It will throw additional light on the latter, to go back, and run the mind over the string of historical facts already stated. Several things will *now* appear less *dark* and *mysterious* than they did *when* they were transpiring. The people were to be left "perfectly free" "subject only to the
18 Constitution." What the *Constitution* had to do with it,

outsiders could not *then* see. Plainly enough *now*, it was an exactly fitted *niche*, for the Dred Scott decision to afterwards come in, and declare the *perfect freedom* of the people, to be just no freedom at all.

Why was the amendment, expressly declaring the right of the people to exclude slavery, voted down? Plainly enough *now*, the adoption of it, would have spoiled the niche for the Dred Scott decision.

Why was the court decision held up? Why, even a Senator's individual opinion withheld, till *after* the presidential election? Plainly enough *now*, the speaking out *then* would have damaged the *"perfectly free"* argument upon which the election was to be carried.

Why the *outgoing* President's felicitation on the indorsement? Why the delay of a re-argument? Why the incoming President's *advance* exhortation in favor of the decision?

These things *look* like the cautious *patting* and *petting* a spirited horse, preparatory to mounting him, when it is dreaded that he may give the rider a fall.

And why the hasty after indorsements of the decision by the President and others?

We can not absolutely *know* that all these exact adaptations are the result of preconcert. But when we see a lot of framed timbers, different portions of which we know have been gotten out at different times and places and by different workmen—Stephen, Franklin, Roger and James, 19 for instance—and when we see these timbers joined together, and see they exactly make the frame of a house or a mill, all the tenons and mortices exactly fitting, and all the lengths and proportions of the different pieces exactly adapted to their respective places, and not a piece too many or too few—not omitting even scaffolding—or, if a single piece be lacking, we can see the place in the frame exactly fitted and prepared to yet bring such piece in—in *such* a case, we find it impossible to not *believe* that Stephen and Franklin and Roger and James all understood one another from the beginning, and all worked upon a common *plan* or *draft* drawn up before the first lick was struck.

It should not be overlooked that, by the Nebraska bill, the people of a *state* as well as *territory*, were to be left *"perfectly free"* *"subject only to the Constitution."*

Why mention a *state*? They were legislating for *territories*, and not *for* or *about* states. Certainly the people of a state *are* and *ought to be* subject to the Constitution of the United States; but why is mention of this *lugged* into this merely *territorial* law? Why are the people of a *territory* and the people of a *state* therein *lumped* together, and their relation to the Constitution therein treated as being *precisely* the same?

While the opinion of *the court*, by Chief Justice Taney, in the Dred Scott case, and the separate opinions of all 20 the concurring judges, expressly declare that the Constitution of the United States neither permits Congress nor a territorial legislature to exclude slavery from any United States territory, they all *omit* to declare whether or not the same Constitution permits a *state*, or the people of a state, to exclude it.

Possibly, this was a mere *omission;* but who can be *quite* sure, if McLean or Curtis had sought to get into the opinion a declaration of unlimited power in the people of a *state* to exclude slavery from their limits, just as Chase and Macy sought to get such declaration, in behalf of the people of a territory, into the Nebraska bill—I ask, who can be quite *sure* that it would not have been voted down, in the one case, as it had been in the other.

The nearest approach to the point of declaring the power of a state over slavery, is made by Judge Nelson. He approaches it more than once, using the precise idea, and *almost* the language too, of the Nebraska act. On one occasion his exact language is, "except in cases where the power is restrained by the Constitution of the United States, the law of the state is supreme over the subject of slavery within its jurisdiction."

In what *cases* the power of the *states* is so restrained by the U. S. Constitution, is left an *open* question, precisely as the same question, as to the restraint on the power of the *territories* was left open in the Nebraska act. Put *that* and *that* together, and we have another nice little niche, which we may, ere long, see filled with another Supreme

Court decision, declaring that the Constitution of the United States does not permit a *state* to exclude slavery from its limits.

And this may especially be expected if the doctrine of "care not whether slavery be voted *down* or voted *up*," shall gain upon the public mind sufficiently to give promise that such a decision can be maintained when made.

Such a decision is all that slavery now lacks of being alike lawful in all the states.

Welcome or unwelcome, such decision *is* probably coming, and will soon be upon us, unless the power of the present political dynasty shall be met and overthrown.

We shall *lie down* pleasantly dreaming that the people of *Missouri* are on the verge of making their state *free;* and we shall *awake* to the *reality,* instead, that the *Supreme* Court has made *Illinois* a *slave* state.

To meet and overthrow the power of that dynasty, is the work now before all those who would prevent that consummation.

That is *what* we have to do.

But *how* can we best do it?

There are those who denounce us *openly* to their *own* friends, and yet whisper *us softly,* that *Senator Douglas* is the *aptest* instrument there is, with which to effect that object. *They* do *not* tell us, nor has *he* told us, that he *wishes* any such object to be effected. They wish us to *in-*
22 *fer* all, from the facts, that he now has a little quarrel with

the present head of the dynasty; and that he has regularly voted with us, on a single point, upon which, he and we, have never differed.

They remind us that *he* is a very *great man,* and that the largest of *us* are very small ones. Let this be granted. But "a *living dog* is better than a *dead lion.*" Judge Douglas, if not a *dead* lion *for this work,* [is] at least a *caged* and *toothless* one. How can he oppose the advances of slavery? He don't *care* anything about it. His avowed *mission is impressing* the "public heart" to *care* nothing about it.

A leading Douglas Democratic newspaper thinks Douglas' superior talent will be needed to resist the revival of the African slave trade.

Does Douglas believe an effort to revive that trade is approaching? He has not said so. Does he *really* think so? But if it is, how can he resist it? For years he has labored to prove it a *sacred right* of white men to take Negro slaves into the new territories. Can he possibly show that it is *less* a sacred right to *buy* them where they can be bought cheapest? And, unquestionably they can be bought *cheaper in Africa* than in *Virginia.*

He has done all in his power to reduce the whole question of slavery to one of a mere *right of property;* and as such, how can *he* oppose the foreign slave trade—how can he refuse that trade in that "property" shall be "perfectly free"—unless he does it as a *protection* to the home production? And as the home *producers* will probably not *ask* 23 the protection, he will be wholly without a ground of opposition.

Senator Douglas holds, we know, that a man may rightfully be *wiser today* than he was *yesterday*—that he may rightfully *change* when he finds himself wrong.

But, can we for that reason, run ahead, and *infer* that he *will* make any particular change, of which he, himself, has given no intimation? Can we *safely* base *our* action upon any such *vague* inference?

Now, as ever, I wish to not *misrepresent* Judge Douglas' *position*, question his *motives*, or do ought that can be personally offensive to him.

Whenever, *if ever*, he and we can come together on *principle* so that *our great cause* may have assistance from *his great ability*, I hope to have interposed no adventitious obstacle.

But clearly, he is not *now* with us—he does not *pretend* to be—he does not *promise* to *ever* be.

Our cause, then, must be intrusted to, and conducted by its own undoubted friends—those whose hands are free, whose hearts are in the work—who *do care* for the result.

Two years ago the Republicans of the nation mustered over thirteen hundred thousand strong.

We did this under the single impulse of resistance to a common danger, with every external circumstance against us.

Of *strange*, *discordant*, and even, *hostile* elements, we gathered from the four winds, and *formed* and fought the battle through, under the constant hot fire of a disciplined, proud, and pampered enemy.

Did we brave all *then*, to *falter* now?—*now*—when that same enemy is *wavering*, dissevered and belligerent?

The result is not doubtful. We shall not fail—if we stand firm, we shall not fail.

Wise counsels may *accelerate* or *mistakes delay* it, but, sooner or later, the victory is *sure* to come.

Speech in reply to Stephen A. Douglas at
Chicago, Illinois:
July 10, 1858

My Fellow-Citizens:—

On yesterday evening, upon the occasion of the reception given to Senator Douglas, I was furnished with a seat very convenient for hearing him, and was otherwise very courteously treated by him and by his friends, and for which I thank him and them. During the course of his remarks my name was mentioned in such a way, as I suppose renders it at least not improper that I should make some sort of reply to him. I shall not attempt to follow him in the precise order in which he addressed the assembled multitude upon that occasion, though I shall perhaps do so in the main. . . .

Judge Douglas makes two points upon my recent speech at Springfield. He says they are to be the issues of this campaign. The first one of these points he bases upon the language in a speech which I delivered at Springfield, which I believe I can quote correctly from memory. I said there that "we are now far into the fifth year since a policy was instituted for the avowed object and with the confident promise of putting an end to slavery agitation; under the operation of that policy, that agitation had [not?] only not ceased, but has constantly augmented. I believe it will not cease until a crisis shall have been reached and passed. A house divided against itself cannot stand. I believe this government cannot endure permanently half slave and half free. I do not expect the Union to be dissolved,"—I am quoting from my speech—"I do not expect the house to fall, but I do expect it will cease to be divided. It will become all one thing or all the other. Either the opponents of slavery will arrest the spread of it, and place it where the public mind shall rest in the belief that it is in the course of ultimate extinction, or its advocates will push it forward until it shall become alike lawful in all the States North as well as South."

What is the paragraph? In this paragraph which I have quoted in your hearing, and to which I ask the attention of all, Judge Douglas thinks he discovers great political heresy. I want your attention particularly to what he has inferred from it. He says I am in favor of making all the States of this Union uniform in all their internal regulations; that in all their domestic concerns I am in favor of making them entirely uniform. He draws this inference from the language I have quoted to you. He says that I am in favor of making war by the North upon the South for the extinction of slavery; that I am also in favor of inviting, as he expresses it, the South to a war upon the North for the purpose of nationalizing salvery. Now, it is singular enough, if you will carefully read that passage over, that I did not say that I was in favor of anything in it. I only said what I expected would take place. I made a prediction only—it may have been a foolish one perhaps. I did not even say that I desired that slavery should be put in course of ultimate extinction. I do say so now, however, so there need be no longer any difficulty about that. It may be written down in the next speech.

Gentlemen, Judge Douglas informed you that this speech of mine was probably carefully prepared. I admit that it was. I am not master of language; I have not a fine education; I am not capable of entering into a disquisition upon dialectics, as I believe you call it; but I do not believe the language I employed bears any such construction as Judge Douglas put upon it. But I don't care about a quibble in regard to words. I know what I meant, and I will not leave this crowd in doubt, if I can explain it to them, what I really meant in the use of that paragraph.

I am not, in the first place, unaware that this Government has endured eighty-two years, half slave and half free. I know that. I am tolerably well acquainted with the history of the country, and I know that it has endured eighty-two years, half slave and half free. I *believe*—and that is what I meant to allude to there—I *believe* it has endured because, during all that time, until the introduction of the Nebraska Bill, the public mind did rest, all the time, in the belief that slavery was in course of ultimate extinction. That was what gave us the rest that we had through that period of eighty-two years;—at least, so I believe. I have always hated slavery, I think, as much as any Abolitionist. I have been an Old Line Whig. I have always hated it, but I have always been quiet about it until this new era of the introduction of the Nebraska Bill began. I always believed that everybody was against it, and that it was in course of ultimate extinction. (Pointing to Mr. Browning, who stood near by,) Browning thought so; the great mass of the nation have rested in the belief that slavery was in course of ultimate extinction. They had reason so to believe.

The adoption of the Constitution and its attendant history led the people to believe so; and that such was the belief of the framers of the Constitution itself. Why did those old men, about the time of the adoption of the Constitution, decree that slavery should not go into the new Territory, where it had not already gone? Why declare that within twenty years the African Slave Trade, by which slaves are supplied, might be cut off by Congress? Why were all these acts? I might enumerate more of such acts—but enough. What were they but a clear indication that the framers of the Constitution intended and expected the ultimate extinction of that institution? And now when I say, as I say in this speech, that Judge Douglas has quoted from, when I say that I think the opponents of slavery will resist the farther spread of it, and place it where the public mind shall rest with the belief that it is in course of ultimate extinction, I only mean to say, that they will place it where the founders of this government originally placed it.

I have said a hundred times, and I have now no inclination to take it back, that I believe there is no right, and ought to be no inclination, in the people of the free States to enter into the slave States, and interfere with the question of slavery at all. I have said that always. Judge Douglas has heard me say it—if not quite a hundred times, at least as good as a hundred times; and when it is said that I am in favor of interfering with slavery where it exists, I know it is unwarranted by anything I have ever *intended*, and, as I believe, by anything I have ever *said*. If, by any means, I have ever used language which could fairly be so construed, (as, however, I believe I never have,) I now correct it.

So much, then, for the inference that Judge Douglas draws, that I am in favor of setting the sections at war with one another. I know that I never meant any such thing, and I believe that no fair mind can infer any such thing from anything I have ever said.

Now, in relation to his inference that I am in favor of a general consolidation of all the local institutions of the various States. I will attend to that for a little while, and try to inquire if I can how on earth it could be that any man could draw such an inference from anything I said. I have said, very many times, in Judge Douglas' hearing, 30 that no man believed more than I in the principle of self-government; that it lies at the bottom of all my ideas of just government from beginning to end. I have denied that his use of that term applies properly. But for the thing itself I deny that any man has ever gone ahead of me in his devotion to the principle, whatever he may have done in efficiency in advocating it. I think that I have said it in your hearing—that I believe each individual is naturally entitled to do as he pleases with himself and the fruit of his labor, so far as it in no wise interferes with any other man's rights, that each community, as a State, has a right to do exactly as it pleases with all the concerns within that State that interfere with the rights of no other State, and that the general government, upon principle, has no right to interfere with any thing other than that general class of things that does concern the whole. I have said that at all times. I have said, as illustrations, that I do not believe in the right of Illinois to interfere with the cranberry laws of Indiana, the oyster laws of Virginia, or the Liquor Laws of Maine. I have said these things over and over again and I repeat them here as my sentiments.

How is it, then, that Judge Douglas infers, because I hope to see slavery put where the public mind shall rest in the belief that it is in the course of ultimate extinction, that I am in favor of Illinois going over and interfering with the cranberry laws of Indiana? What can authorize him to draw any such inference? I suppose there might be one thing that at least enabled *him* to draw such an inference that would 31 not be true with me or with many others—that is, because he looks upon all this matter of slavery as an exceedingly little thing—this matter of keeping one sixth of the population of the whole nation in a state of oppression and tyranny unequalled in the world. He looks upon it as being an exceedingly little thing—only equal to the question of the cranberry laws of Indiana—as something having no moral question in it—as something on a par with the question of whether a man shall pasture his land with cattle, or plant it with tobacco—so little and so small a thing, that he concludes if I could desire that anything should be done to bring about the ultimate extinction of that little thing, I must be in favor of bringing about an amalgamation of all the other little things in the Union. Now, it so happens— and there, I presume, is the foundation of this mistake—that the Judge thinks thus; and it so happens that there is a vast portion of the American people that do *not* look upon that matter as being this very little thing. They look upon it as a vast moral evil; they can prove it is such by the writings of those who gave us the blessings of liberty which we enjoy, and that they so looked upon it and not as an evil merely confining itself to the States where it is situated; and while we agree that, by the Constitution we assented to, in the States where it exists we have no right to interfere with it because it is in the Constitution and we are by both duty and inclination to stick by that Constitution in all its letter and spirit from beginning to end.

So much then as to my disposition—my wish—to have all the State legislatures blotted out, and to have one general consolidated government, and a uniformity of domestic regulations in all the States, by which I suppose it is meant if we raise corn here, we must make sugar-cane grow here too, and we must make those which grow North, grow in the South. All this I suppose the Judge understands I am in favor of doing. Now, so much for all this nonsense—for I must call it so. The Judge can have no issue with me on a question of establishing uniformity in the domestic regulations of the States.

A little now on the other point—the Dred Scott Decision. Another one of the issues he says that is to be made with me, is upon his devotion to the Dred Scott Decision, and my opposition to it.

I have expressed heretofore, and I now repeat, my opposition to the Dred Scott Decision, but I should be allowed to state the nature of that opposition, and I ask your indulgence while I do so. What is fairly implied by the term Judge Douglas has used, "resistance to the Decision?" I do not resist it. If I wanted to take Dred Scott from his master, I would be interfering with property, and that terrible difficulty that Judge Douglas speaks of, of interfering with property, would arise. But I am doing no such thing as that, but all that I am doing is refusing to obey it as a political rule. If I were in Congress, and a vote should come up on a question whether slavery should be prohibited in a new Territory, in spite of that Dred Scott Decision, I would vote that it should.

That is what I would do. Judge Douglas said last night, that before the Decision he might advance his opinion, and it might be contrary to the decision when it was made; but *after* it was made he would abide by it until it was reversed. Just so! We let this property abide by the decision, but we will try to reverse that decision. We will try to put it where Judge Douglas would not object, for he says he will obey it until it is reversed. Somebody has to reverse that decision, since it is made, and we mean to reverse it, and we mean to do it peaceably.

What are the uses of decisions of courts? They have two uses. As rules of property they have two uses. First— they decide upon the question before the court. They decide in this case that Dred Scott is a slave. Nobody resists that. Not only that, but they say to everybody else, that persons standing just as Dred Scott stands, are as he is. That is, they say that when a question comes up upon another person it will be so decided again, unless the court decides another way, unless the court overrules its decision. Well, we mean to do what we can to have the court decide the other way. That is one thing we mean to try to do. . . .

Now, it happens that we meet together once every year, sometimes about the 4th of July, for some reason or 34 other. These 4th of July gatherings, I suppose, have their uses. If you will indulge me, I will state what I suppose to be some of them.

We are now a mighty nation, we are thirty—or about thirty millions of people, and we own and inhabit about one-fifteenth part of the dry land of the whole earth. We run our memory back over the pages of history for about eighty-two years, and we discover that we were then a very small people in point of numbers, vastly inferior to what we are now, with a vastly less extent of country,— with vastly less of everything we deem desirable among men,—we look upon the change as exceedingly advantageous to us and to our posterity, and we fix upon something that happened away back, as in some way or other being connected with this rise of prosperity. We find a race of men living in that day whom we claim as our fathers and grandfathers; they were iron men; they fought for the principle that they were contending for; and we understand that by what they then did it has followed that the degree of prosperity that we now enjoy has come to us. We hold this annual celebration to remind ourselves of all the good done in this process of time, of how it was done and who did it, and how we are historically connected with it; and we go from these meetings in better humor with ourselves—we feel more attached the one to the other, and more firmly bound to the country we inhabit. In every way we are better men in the age, and race, and country in which we live, for these celebrations. 35

But after we have done all this we have not yet reached the whole. There is something else connected with it. We have besides these men—descended by blood from our ancestors—among us perhaps half our people who are not descendants at all of these men, they are men who have come from Europe—German, Irish, French and Scandinavian—men that have come from Europe themselves, or whose ancestors have come hither and settled here, finding themselves our equals in all things. If they look back through this history to trace their connection with those days by blood, they find they have none, they cannot carry themselves back into that glorious epoch and make themselves feel that they are part of us, but when they look through that old Declaration of Independence, they find that those old men say that "We hold these truths to be self-evident, that all men are created equal," and then they feel that that moral sentiment taught in that day evidences their relation to those men, that it is the father of all moral principle in them, and that they have a right to claim it as though they were blood of the blood, and flesh of the flesh, of the men who wrote that Declaration, and so they are. That is the electric cord in that Declaration that links the hearts of patriotic and liberty-loving men together, that will link those patriotic hearts as long as the love of freedom exists in the minds of men throughout the world.

36   Now, sirs, for the purpose of squaring things with this

idea of "don't care if slavery is voted up or voted down," for sustaining the Dred Scot Decision, for holding that the Declaration of Independence did not mean anything at all, we have Judge Douglas giving his exposition of what the Declaration of Independence means, and we have him saying that the people of America were equal to the people of England. According to his construction, you Germans are not connected with it. Now, I ask you in all soberness, if all these things, if indulged in, if ratified, if confirmed and endorsed, if taught to our children and repeated to them, do not tend to rub out the sentiment of liberty in the country, and to transform this government into a government of some other form. These arguments that are made, that the inferior race are to be treated with as much allowance as they are capable of enjoying; that as much is to be done for them as their condition will allow. What are these arguments? They are the arguments that kings have made for enslaving the people in all ages of the world. You will find that all the arguments in favor of kingcraft were of this class; they always bestrode the necks of the people, not that they wanted to do it, but because the people were better off for being ridden. That is their argument, and this argument of the Judge is the same old serpent that says, you work, and I eat, you toil, and I will enjoy the fruits of it. Turn it whatever way you will—whether it come from the mouth of a King, an excuse for enslaving the people of his country, or from the 37 mouth of men of one race as a reason for enslaving the men of another race, it is all the same old serpent, and I hold if that course of argumentation that is made for the purpose of convincing the public mind that we should not care about this, should be granted, it does not stop with the negro. I should like to know if taking this old Declaration of Independence, which declares that all men are equal upon principle, and making exceptions to it, where will it stop? If one man says it does not mean a negro, why may not another say it does not mean some other man? If that Declaration is not the truth, let us get the Statute book in which we find it and tear it out! Who is so bold as to do it! If it is not true let us tear it out! (cries of "no, no,") Let us stick to it then. (cheers) Let us stand firmly by it then. (applause)

It may be argued that there are certain conditions that make necessities and impose them upon us, and to the extent that a necessity is imposed upon a man, he must submit to it. I think that was the condition in which we found ourselves when we established this government. We had slavery among us, we could not get our Constitution unless we permitted them to remain in slavery, we could not secure the good we did secure if we grasped for more, and having by necessity submitted to that much, it does not destroy the principle that is the charter of our liberties. Let that charter stand as our standard.

38   My friend has said to me that I am a poor hand to

quote Scripture. I will try it again, however. It is said in one of the admonitions of the Lord, "As your Father in heaven is perfect, be ye also perfect." The Saviour, I suppose, did not expect that any human creature could be perfect as the Father in Heaven; but He said, "As your Father in Heaven is perfect, be ye also perfect." He set that up as a standard, and he who did most towards reaching that standard, attained the highest degree of moral perfection. So I say in relation to the principle that all men are created equal, let it be as nearly reached as we can. If we cannot give freedom to every creature, let us do nothing that will impose slavery upon any other creature. Let us then turn this government back into the channel in which the framers of the Constitution originally placed it. Let us stand firmly by each other. If we do not do so, we are turning in the contrary direction, that our friend Judge Douglas proposes—not intentionally—as working in the traces that tend to make this one universal Slave Nation. He is one that runs in that direction, and as such I resist him.

My friends, I have detained you about as long as I desired to do, and I have only to say, let us discard all this quibbling about this man and the other man—this race and that race and the other race being inferior, and therefore they must be placed in an inferior position—discarding our standard that we have left us. Let us discard all these things, and unite as 39 one people throughout this land, until we shall once more stand up declaring that all men are created equal.

My friends, I could not, without launching off upon some new topic, which would detain you too long, continue to-night. I thank you for this most extensive audience that you have furnished me to-night. I leave you, hoping that the lamp of liberty will burn in your bosoms until there shall no longer be a doubt that all men are created free and equal.

Address at Cooper Institute, New York: February 27, 1860

Mr. President and fellow-citizens of New York:—

The facts with which I shall deal this evening are mainly old and familiar; nor is there anything new in the general use I shall make of them. If there shall be any novelty, it will be in the mode of presenting the facts, and the inferences and observations following that presentation.

In his speech last autumn, at Columbus, Ohio, as reported in "The New-York Times," Senator Douglas said:

"Our fathers, when they framed the Government under which we live, understood this question just as well, and even better, than we do now."

I fully indorse this, and I adopt it as a text for this discourse. I so adopt it because it furnishes a precise and an agreed starting point for a discussion between Republicans and that wing of the Democracy headed by Senator Douglas. It simply leaves the inquiry: *"What was the understanding those fathers had of the question mentioned?"*

What is the frame of government under which we live? 41

The answer must be: "The Constitution of the United States." That Constitution consists of the original, framed in 1787, (and under which the present government first went into operation,) and twelve subsequently framed amendments, the first ten of which were framed in 1789.

Who were our fathers that framed the Constitution? I suppose the "thirty-nine" who signed the original instrument may be fairly called our fathers who framed that part of the present Government. It is almost exactly true to say they framed it, and it is altogether true to say they fairly represented the opinion and sentiment of the whole nation at that time. Their names, being familiar to nearly all, and accessible to quite all, need not now be repeated.

I take these "thirty-nine," for the present, as being "our fathers who framed the Government under which we live."

What is the question which, according to the text, those fathers understood "just as well, and even better than we do now?"

It is this: Does the proper division of local from federal authority, or anything in the Constitution, forbid our *Federal Government* to control as to slavery in *our Federal Territories*?

Upon this, Senator Douglas holds the affirmative, and Republicans the negative. This affirmation and denial form an issue; and this issue—this question—is precisely what the text declares our fathers understood "better than we."

Let us now inquire whether the "thirty-nine," or any of them, ever acted upon this question; and if they did, how they acted upon it—how they expressed that better understanding?

In 1784, three years before the Constitution—the United States then owning the Northwestern Territory, and no other, the Congress of the Confederation had before them the question of prohibiting slavery in that Territory; and four of the "thirty-nine" who afterward framed the Constitution, were in that Congress, and voted on that question. Of these, Roger Sherman, Thomas Mifflin, and Hugh Williamson voted for the prohibition, thus showing that, in their understanding, no line dividing local from federal authority, nor anything else, properly forbade the Federal Government to control as to slavery in federal territory. The other of the four—James M'Henry—voted against the prohibition, showing that, for some cause, he thought it improper to vote for it.

In 1787, still before the Constitution, but while the Convention was in session framing it, and while the Northwestern Territory still was the only territory owned by the United States, the same question of prohibiting slavery in the territory again came before the Congress of the Confederation; and two more of the "thirty-nine" who afterward signed the Constitution, were in that Congress, and voted on the question. They were William Blount and William Few; and they both voted for the prohibition—thus showing that, in their understanding, no line dividing local from federal authority, nor anything else, properly forbids the Federal Government to control as to slavery in Federal territory. This time the prohibition became a law, being part of what is now well known as the Ordinance of '87.

The question of federal control of slavery in the territories, seems not to have been directly before the Convention which framed the original Constitution; and hence it is not recorded that the "thirty-nine," or any of them, while engaged on that instrument, expressed any opinion on that precise question.

In 1789, by the first Congress which sat under the Constitution, an act was passed to enforce the Ordinance of '87, including the prohibition of slavery in the Northwestern Territory. The bill for this act was reported by one of the "thirty-nine," Thomas Fitzsimmons, then a member of the House of Representatives from Pennsylvania. It went through all its stages without a word of opposition, and finally passed both branches without yeas and nays, which is equivalent to an unanimous passage. In this Congress there were sixteen of the thirty-nine fathers who framed the original Constitution. They were John

Langdon, Nicholas Gilman, Wm. S. Johnson, Roger Sherman, Robert Morris, Thos. Fitzsimmons, William Few, Abraham Baldwin, Rufus King, William Paterson, George Clymer, Richard Bassett, George Reed, Pierce Butler, Daniel Carroll, James Madison.

This shows that, in their understanding, no line dividing local from federal authority, nor anything in the Constitution, properly forbade Congress to prohibit slavery in the federal territory; else both their fidelity to correct principle, and their oath to support the Constitution, would have constrained them to oppose the prohibition.

Again, George Washington, another of the "thirty-nine," was then President of the United States, and, as such approved and signed the bill; thus completing its validity as a law, and thus showing that, in his understanding, no line dividing local from federal authority, nor anything in the Constitution, forbade the Federal Government, to control as to slavery in federal territory.

No great while after the adoption of the original Constitution, North Carolina ceded to the Federal Government the country now constituting the State of Tennessee; and a few years later Georgia ceded that which now constitutes the States of Mississippi and Alabama. In both deeds of cession it was made a condition by the ceding States that the Federal Government should not prohibit slavery in the ceded country. Besides this, slavery was then actually in the ceded country. Under these circumstances, Congress, on taking charge of these countries, did not absolutely prohibit slavery within them. But they did interfere with it—take control of it—even there, to a certain extent. In 1798, Congress organized the Territory of Mississippi. In the act of organization, they prohibited the bringing of slaves into the Territory, from any place without the United States, by fine, and giving freedom to slaves so brought. This act passed both branches of Congress with yeas and nays. In that Congress were three of the "thirty-nine" who framed the original Constitution. They were John Langdon, George Read and Abraham Baldwin. They all, probably, voted for it. Certainly they would have placed their opposition to it upon record, if, in their understanding, any line dividing local from federal authority, or anything in the Constitution, properly forbade the Federal Government to control as to slavery in federal territory.

In 1803, the Federal Government purchased the Louisiana country. Our former territorial acquisitions came from certain of our own States; but this Louisiana country was acquired from a foreign nation. In 1804, Congress gave a territorial organization to that part of it which now constitutes the State of Louisiana. New Orleans, lying within that part, was an old and comparatively large city. There were other considerable towns and settlements, and slavery was extensively and thoroughly intermingled with the people. Congress did not, in the Territorial Act, prohibit slavery; but they did interfere with it—take control of it—in a more marked and extensive way than they did in the case of Mississippi. The substance of the provision therein made, in relation to slaves, was:

First. That no slave should be imported into the territory from foreign parts.

Second. That no slave should be carried into it who had been imported into the United States since the first day of May, 1798.

Third. That no slave should be carried into it, except by the owner, and for his own use as a settler; the penalty in all the cases being a fine upon the violator of the law, and freedom to the slave.

This act also was passed without yeas and nays. In the Congress which passed it, there were two of the "thirty-nine." They were Abraham Baldwin and Jonathan Dayton. As stated in the case of Mississippi, it is probable they both voted for it. They would not have allowed it to pass without recording their opposition to it, if, in their understanding, it violated either the line properly dividing local from federal authority, or any provision of the Constitution.

In 1819–20, came and passed the Missouri question. Many votes were taken, by yeas and nays, in both branches of Congress, upon the various phases of the general question. Two of the "thirty-nine"—Rufus King and Charles Pinckney—were members of that Congress. Mr. King steadily voted for slavery prohibition and against all compromises, while Mr. Pinckney as steadily voted against slavery prohibition and against all compromises. By this, Mr. King showed that, in his understanding, no line dividing local from federal authority, nor anything in the Constitution, was violated by Congress prohibiting slavery in federal territory; while Mr. Pinckney, by his votes, showed that, in his understanding, there was some sufficient reason for opposing such prohibition in that case.

The cases I have mentioned are the only acts of the "thirty-nine," or of any of them, upon the direct issue, which I have been able to discover.

To enumerate the persons who thus acted, as being four in 1784, two in 1787, seventeen in 1789, three in 1798, two in 1804, and two in 1819–20—there would be thirty of them. But this would be counting John Langdon, Roger Sherman, William Few, Rufus King, and George Read each twice, and Abraham Baldwin, three times. The true number of those of the "thirty-nine" whom I have shown to have acted upon the question, which, by the text, they understood better than we, is twenty-three, leaving sixteen not shown to have acted upon it in any way.

Here, then, we have twenty-three out of our thirty-nine
48 fathers "who framed the government under which we

live," who have, upon their official responsibility and their corporal oaths, acted upon the very question which the text affirms they "understood just as well, and even better than we do now;" and twenty-one of them—a clear majority of the whole "thirty-nine"—so acting upon it as to make them guilty of gross political impropriety and wilful perjury, if, in their understanding, any proper division between local and federal authority, or anything in the Constitution they had made themselves, and sworn to support, forbade the Federal Government to control as to slavery in the federal territories. Thus the twenty-one acted; and, as actions speak louder than words, so actions, under such responsibility, speak still louder.

Two of the twenty-three voted against Congressional prohibition of slavery in the federal territories, in the instances in which they acted upon the question. But for what reasons they so voted is not known. They may have done so because they thought a proper division of local from federal authority, or some provision or principle of the Constitution, stood in the way; or they may, without any such question, have voted against the prohibition, on what appeared to them to be sufficient grounds of expediency. No one who has sworn to support the Constitution can conscientiously vote for what he understands to be an unconstitutional measure, however expedient he may think it; but one may and ought to vote against a measure which he deems constitutional, if, at the same 49 time, he deems it inexpedient. It, therefore, would be unsafe to set down even the two who voted against the prohibition, as having done so because, in their understanding, any proper division of local from federal authority, or anything in the Constitution, forbade the Federal Government to control as to slavery in federal territory.

The remaining sixteen of the "thirty-nine," so far as I have discovered, have left no record of their understanding upon the direct question of federal control of slavery in the federal territories. But there is much reason to believe that their understanding upon that question would not have appeared different from that of their twenty-three compeers, had it been manifested at all.

For the purpose of adhering rigidly to the text, I have purposely omitted whatever understanding may have been manifested by any person, however distinguished, other than the thirty-nine fathers who framed the original Constitution; and, for the same reason, I have also omitted whatever understanding may have been manifested by any of the "thirty-nine" even, on any other phase of the general question of slavery. If we should look into their acts and declarations on those other phases, as the foreign slave trade, and the morality and policy of slavery generally, it would appear to us that on the direct question of federal control of slavery in federal territories, the sixteen, if they had acted at all, would probably have acted just as 50 the twenty-three did. Among that sixteen were several of the most noted anti-slavery men of those times—as Dr. Franklin, Alexander Hamilton and Gouverneur Morris—while there was not one now known to have been otherwise, unless it may be John Rutledge, of South Carolina.

The sum of the whole is, that of our thirty-nine fathers who framed the original Constitution, twenty-one—a clear majority of the whole—certainly understood that no proper division of local from federal authority, nor any part of the Constitution, forbade the Federal Government to control slavery in the federal territories; while all the rest probably had the same understanding. Such, unquestionably, was the understanding of our fathers who framed the original Constitution; and the text affirms that they understood the question "better than we."

But, so far, I have been considering the understanding of the question manifested by the framers of the original Constitution. In and by the original instrument, a mode was provided for amending it; and, as I have already stated, the present frame of "the Government under which we live" consists of that original, and twelve amendatory articles framed and adopted since. Those who now insist that federal control of slavery in federal territories violates the Constitution, point us to the provisions which they suppose it thus violates; and, as I understand, that all fix upon provisions in these amendatory articles, and not in the original instrument. The Supreme Court, in the Dred Scott case, plant themselves upon the 51 fifth amendment, which provides that no person shall be deprived of "life, liberty or property without due process of law;" while Senator Douglas and his peculiar adherents plant themselves upon the tenth amendment, providing that "the powers not delegated to the United States by the Constitution" "are reserved to the States respectively, or to the people."

Now, it so happens that these amendments were framed by the first Congress which sat under the Constitution—the identical Congress which passed the act already mentioned, enforcing the prohibition of slavery in the Northwestern Territory. Not only was it the same Congress, but they were the identical, same individual men who, at the same session, and at the same time within the session, had under consideration, and in progress toward maturity, these Constitutional amendments, and this act prohibiting slavery in all the territory the nation then owned. The Constitutional amendments were introduced before, and passed after the act enforcing the Ordinance of '87; so that, during the whole pendency of the act to enforce the Ordinance, the Constitutional amendments were also pending.

The seventy-six members of that Congress, including sixteen of the framers of the original Constitution, as before stated, were pre-eminently our fathers who framed that part of "the Government under which we live," which is now claimed as forbidding the Federal Government to control slavery in the federal territories.

Is it not a little presumptuous in any one at this day to affirm that the two things which that Congress deliberately framed, and carried to maturity at the same time, are absolutely inconsistent with each other? And does not such affirmation become impudently absurd when coupled with the other affirmation from the same mouth, that those who did the two things, alleged to be inconsistent, understood whether they really were inconsistent better than we—better than he who affirms that they are inconsistent?

It is surely safe to assume that the thirty-nine framers of the original Constitution, and the seventy-six members of the Congress which framed the amendments thereto, taken together, do certainly include those who may be fairly called "our fathers who framed the Government under which we live." And so assuming, I defy any man to show that any one of them ever, in his whole life, declared that, in his understanding, any proper division of local from federal authority, or any part of the Constitution, forbade the Federal Government to control as to slavery in the federal territories. I go a step further. I defy any one to show that any living man in the whole world ever did, prior to the beginning of the present century, (and I might almost say prior to the beginning of the last half of the present century,) declare that, in his understanding, any proper division of local from federal authority, or any part of the Constitution, forbade the Federal Government to control as to slavery in the federal territories. To those who now so declare, I give, not only "our fathers who framed the Government under which we live," but with them all other living men within the century in which it was framed, among whom to search, and they shall not be able to find the evidence of a single man agreeing with them.

Now, and here, let me guard a little against being misunderstood. I do not mean to say we are bound to follow implicitly in whatever our fathers did. To do so, would be to discard all the lights of current experience—to reject all progress—all improvement. What I do say is, that if we would supplant the opinions and policy of our fathers in any case, we should do so upon evidence so conclusive, and argument so clear, that even their great authority, fairly considered and weighed, cannot stand; and most surely not in a case whereof we ourselves declare they understood the question better than we.

If any man at this day sincerely believes that a proper division of local from federal authority, or any part of the Constitution, forbids the Federal Government to control as to slavery in the federal territories, he is right to say so, and to enforce his position by all truthful evidence and fair argument which he can. But he has no right to mislead others, who have less access to history, and less leisure to study it, into the false belief that "our fathers who framed the Government under which we live" were of the same opinion—thus substituting falsehood and deception for truthful evidence and fair argument. If any man at this day sincerely believes "our fathers who framed the Government under which we live," used and applied principles, in other cases, which ought to have led them to understand that a proper division of local from federal authority or some part of the Constitution, forbids the Federal Government to control as to slavery in the federal territories, he is right to say so. But he should, at the same time, brave the responsibility of declaring that, in his opinion, he understands their principles better than they did themselves; and especially should he not shirk that responsibility by asserting that they "understood the question just as well, and even better, than we do now."

But enough! *Let all who believe that "our fathers who framed the Government under which we live, understood this question just as well, and even better, than we do now," speak as they spoke, and act as they acted upon it. This is all Republicans ask—all Republicans desire—in relation to slavery. As those fathers marked it, so let it be again marked, as an evil not to be extended, but to be tolerated and protected only because of and so far as its actual presence among us makes that toleration and protection a necessity. Let all the guaranties those fathers gave it, be, not grudgingly, but fully and fairly, maintained.* For this Republicans contend, and with this, so far as I know or believe, they will be content.

And now, if they would listen—as I suppose they will not—I would address a few words to the Southern people.

I would say to them:—You consider yourselves a reasonable and a just people; and I consider that in the general qualities of reason and justice you are not inferior to any other people. Still, when you speak of us Republicans, you do so only to denounce us as reptiles, or, at the best, as no better than outlaws. You will grant a hearing to pirates or murderers, but nothing like it to "Black Republicans." In all your contentions with one another, each of you deems an unconditional condemnation of "Black Republicanism" as the first thing to be attended to. Indeed, such condemnation of us seems to be an indispensable prerequisite—license, so to speak—among you to be admitted or permitted to speak at all. Now, can you, or not, be prevailed upon to pause and to consider whether this is quite just to us, or even to yourselves? Bring forward your charges and specifications, and then be patient long enough to hear us deny or justify.

You say we are sectional. We deny it. That makes an issue; and the burden of proof is upon you. You produce your proof; and what is it? Why, that our party has no existence in your section—gets no votes in your section. 56 The fact is substantially true; but does it prove the issue?

If it does, then in case we should, without change of principle, begin to get votes in your section, we should thereby cease to be sectional. You cannot escape this conclusion; and yet, are you willing to abide by it? If you are, you will probably soon find that we have ceased to be sectional, for we shall get votes in your section this very year. You will then begin to discover, as the truth plainly is, that your proof does not touch the issue. The fact that we got no votes in your section, is a fact of your making, and not of ours. And if there be fault in that fact, that fault is primarily yours, and remains until you show that we repel you by some wrong principle or practice. If we do repel you by any wrong principle or practice, the fault is ours; but this brings you to where you ought to have started—to a discussion of the right or wrong of our principle. If our principle, put in practice, would wrong your section for the benefit of ours, or for any other object, then our principle, and we with it, are sectional, and are justly opposed and denounced as such. Meet us, then, on the question of whether our principle, put in practice, would wrong your section; and so meet it as if it were possible that something may be said on our side. Do you accept the challenge? No! Then you really believe that the principle which "our fathers who framed the Government under which we live" thought so clearly right as to adopt it, and indorse it again and again, upon their official oaths, is in fact so clearly wrong as to demand your condemnation without a moment's consideration.

Some of you delight to flaunt in our faces the warning against sectional parties given by Washington in his Farewell Address. Less than eight years before Washington gave that warning, he had, as President of the United States, approved and signed an act of Congress, enforcing the prohibition of slavery in the Northwestern Territory, which act embodied the policy of the Government upon that subject up to and at the very moment he penned that warning; and about one year after he penned it, he wrote LaFayette that he considered that prohibition a wise measure, expressing in the same connection his hope that we should at some time have a confederacy of free States.

Bearing this in mind, and seeing that sectionalism has since arisen upon this same subject, is that warning a weapon in your hands against us, or in our hands against you? Could Washington himself speak, would he cast the blame of that sectionalism upon us, who sustain his policy, or upon you who repudiate it? We respect that warning of Washington, and we commend it to you, together with his example pointing to the right application of it.

But you say you are conservative—eminently conservative—while we are revolutionary, destructive, or something of the sort. What is conservatism? Is it not adherence to the old and tried, against the new and untried? We stick to, contend for, the identical old policy on the point in controversy which was adopted by "our fathers who framed the Government under which we live;" while you with one accord reject, and scout, and spit upon that old policy, and insist upon substituting something new. True, you disagree among yourself as to what that substitute shall be. You are divided on new propositions and plans, but you are unanimous in rejecting and denouncing the old policy of the fathers. Some of you are for reviving the foreign slave trade; some for a Congressional Slave-Code for the Territories; some for Congress forbidding the Territories to prohibit Slavery within their limits; some for maintaining Slavery in the Territories through the judiciary; some for the "gur-reat pur-rinciple" that "if one man would enslave another, no third man should object," fantastically called "Popular Sovereignty;" but never a man among you is in favor of federal prohibition of slavery in federal territories, according to the practice of "our fathers who framed the Government under which we live." Not one of all your various plans can show a precedent or an advocate in the century within which our Government originated. Consider, then, whether your claim of conservatism for yourselves, and your charge of destructiveness against us, are based on the most clear and stable foundations.

Again, you say we have made the slavery question more prominent than it formerly was. We deny it. We admit that it is more prominent, but we deny that we made it so. It was not we, but you, who discarded the old policy of the fathers. We resisted, and still resist, your innovation; and thence comes the greater prominence of the question. Would you have that question reduced to its former proportions? Go back to that old policy. What has been will be again, under the same conditions. If you would have the peace of the old times, readopt the precepts and policy of the old times.

You charge that we stir up insurrections among your slaves. We deny it; and what is your proof? Harper's Ferry! John Brown!! John Brown was no Republican; and you have failed to implicate a single Republican in his Harper's Ferry enterprise. If any member of our party is guilty in that matter, you know it or you do not know it. If you do know it, you are inexcusable for not designating the man and proving the fact. If you do not know it, you are inexcusable for asserting it, and especially for persisting in the assertion after you have tried and failed to make the proof. You need not be told that persisting in a charge which one does not know to be true, is simply malicious slander.

Some of you admit that no Republican designedly aided or encouraged the Harper's Ferry affair, but still insist that our doctrines and declarations necessarily lead to such results. We do not believe it. We know we hold to no doctrine, and make no declaration, which were not held to and made by "our fathers who framed the Government under which we live." You never dealt fairly by us in relation to this affair. When it occurred, some important

State elections were near at hand, and you were in evident glee with the belief that, by charging the blame upon us, you could get an advantage of us in those elections. The elections came, and your expectations were not quite fulfilled. Every Republican man knew that, as to himself at least, your charge was a slander, and he was not much inclined by it to cast his vote in your favor. Republican doctrines and declarations are accompanied with a continual protest against any interference whatever with your slaves, or with you about your slaves. Surely, this does not encourage them to revolt. True, we do, in common with "our fathers who framed the Government under which we live," declare our belief that slavery is wrong; but the slaves do not hear us declare even this. For anything we say or do, the slaves would scarcely know there is a Republican party. I believe they would not, in fact, generally know it but for your misrepresentations of us, in their hearing. In your political contests among yourselves, each faction charges the other with sympathy with Black Republicanism; and then, to give point to the charge, defines Black Republicanism to simply be insurrection, blood and thunder among the slaves.

Slave insurrections are no more common now than they were before the Republican party was organized. What induced the Southampton insurrection, twenty-eight years ago, in which, at least three times as many lives were lost as at Harper's Ferry? You can scarcely stretch your very 61 elastic fancy to the conclusion that Southampton was "got up by Black Republicanism." In the present state of things in the United States, I do not think a general, or even a very extensive slave insurrection is possible. The indispensable concert of action cannot be attained. The slaves have no means of rapid communication; nor can incendiary freemen, black or white, supply it. The explosive materials are everywhere in parcels; but there neither are, nor can be supplied, the indispensable connecting trains.

Much is said by Southern people about the affection of slaves for their masters and mistresses, and a part of it, at least, is true. A plot for an uprising could scarcely be devised and communicated to twenty individuals before some one of them, to save the life of a favorite master or mistress, would divulge it. This is the rule; and the slave revolution in Hayti was not an exception to it, but a case occurring under peculiar circumstances. The gunpowder plot of British history, though not connected with slaves, was more in point. In that case, only about twenty were admitted to the secret; and yet one of them, in his anxiety to save a friend, betrayed the plot to that friend, and, by consequence, averted the calamity. Occasional poisonings from the kitchen, and open or stealthy assassinations in the field, and local revolts extending to a score or so, will continue to occur as the natural results of slavery; but no 62 general insurrection of slaves, as I think, can happen in this country for a long time. Whoever much fears, or much hopes for such an event, will be alike disappointed.

In the language of Mr. Jefferson, uttered many years ago, "It is still in our power to direct the process of emancipation, and deportation, peaceably, and in such slow degrees, as that the evil will wear off insensibly; and their places by, *pari passu*, filled up by free white laborers. If, on the contrary, it is left to force itself on, human nature must shudder at the prospect held up."

Mr. Jefferson did not mean to say, nor do I, that the power of emancipation is in the Federal Government. He spoke of Virginia; and, as to the power of emancipation, I speak of the slave-holding States only. The Federal Government, however, as we insist, has the power of restraining the extension of the institution—the power to insure that a slave insurrection shall never occur on any American soil which is now free from slavery.

John Brown's effort was peculiar. It was not a slave insurrection. It was an attempt by white men to get up a revolt among slaves, in which the slaves refused to participate. In fact, it was so absurd that the slaves, with all their ignorance, saw plainly enough it could not succeed. That affair, in its philosophy, corresponds with the many attempts, related in history, at the assassination of kings and emperors. An enthusiast broods over the oppression of a people till he fancies himself commissioned by Heaven to liberate them. He ventures the attempt, which 63 ends in little else than his own execution. Orsini's attempt on Louis Napoleon, and John Brown's attempt at Harper's Ferry were, in their philosophy, precisely the same. The eagerness to cast blame on old England in the one case, and on New England in the other, does not disprove the sameness of the two things.

And how much would it avail you, if you could, by the use of John Brown, Helper's Book, and the like, break up the Republican organization? Human action can be modified to some extent, but human nature cannot be changed. There is a judgment and a feeling against slavery in this nation, which cast at least a million and a half votes. You cannot destroy that judgment and feeling—that sentiment—by breaking up the political organization which rallies around it. You can scarcely scatter and disperse an army which has been formed into order in the face of your heaviest fire; but if you could, how much would you gain by forcing the sentiment which created it out of the peaceful channel of the ballot-box, into some other channel? What would that other channel probably be? Would the number of John Browns be lessened or enlarged by the operation?

But you will break up the Union rather than submit to a denial of your Constitutional rights.

That has a somewhat reckless sound; but it would be palliated, if not fully justified, were we proposing, by the 64 mere force of numbers, to deprive you of some right, plainly written down in the Constitution. But we are proposing no such thing.

When you make these declarations, you have a specific and well-understood allusion to an assumed Constitutional right of yours, to take slaves into the federal territories, and to hold them there as property. But no such right is specifically written in the Constitution. That instrument is literally silent about any such right. We, on the contrary, deny that such a right has any existence in the Constitution, even by implication.

Your purpose, then, plainly stated, is that you will destroy the Government, unless you be allowed to construe and enforce the Constitution as you please, on all points in dispute between you and us. You will rule or ruin in all events.

This, plainly stated, is your language. Perhaps you will say the Supreme Court has decided the disputed Constitutional question in your favor. Not quite so. But waiving the lawyer's distinction between dictum and decision, the Court have decided the question for you in a sort of way. The Court have substantially said, it is your Constitutional right to take slaves into the federal territories, and to hold them there as property. When I say the decision was made in a sort of way, I mean it was made in a divided Court, by a bare majority of the Judges, and they not quite agreeing with one another in the reasons for making it; that it is so made as that its avowed supporters 65 disagree with one another about its meaning, and that it was mainly based upon a mistaken statement of fact—the statement in the opinion that "the right of property in a slave is distinctly and expressly affirmed in the Constitution."

An inspection of the Constitution will show that the right of property in a slave is not *"distinctly* and *expressly* affirmed" in it. Bear in mind, the Judges do not pledge their judicial opinion that such right is *impliedly* affirmed in the Constitution; but they pledge their veracity that it is *"distinctly* and *expressly"* affirmed there—"distinctly," that is, not mingled with anything else—"expressly," that is, in words meaning just that, without the aid of any inference, and susceptible of no other meaning.

If they had only pledged their judicial opinion that such right is affirmed in the instrument by implication, it would be open to others to show that neither the word "slave" nor "slavery" is to be found in the Constitution, nor the word "property" even, in any connection with language alluding to the things slave, or slavery; and that wherever in that instrument the slave is alluded to, he is called a "person;"— and wherever his master's legal right in relation to him is alluded to, it is spoken of as "service or labor which may be due,"—as a debt payable in service or labor. Also, it would be open to show, by contemporaneous history, that 66 this mode of alluding to slaves and slavery, instead of speaking of them, was employed on purpose to exclude from the Constitution the idea that there could be property in man.

To show all this, is easy and certain.

When this obvious mistake of the Judges shall be brought to their notice, is it not reasonable to expect that they will withdraw the mistaken statement, and reconsider the conclusion based upon it?

And then it is to be remembered that "our fathers, who framed the Government under which we live"—the men who made the Constitution—decided this same Constitutional question in our favor, long ago—decided it without division among themselves, when making the decision; without division among themselves about the meaning of it after it was made, and, so far as any evidence is left, without basing it upon any mistaken statement of facts.

Under all these circumstances, do you really feel yourselves justified to break up this Government unless such a court decision as yours is, shall be at once submitted to as a conclusive and final rule of political action? But you will not abide the election of a Republican president! In that supposed event, you say, you will destroy the Union; and then, you say, the great crime of having destroyed it will be upon us! That is cool. A highwayman holds a pistol to my ear, and mutters through his teeth, "Stand and deliver, or I shall kill you, and then you will be a murderer!"

To be sure, what the robber demanded of me—my

money—was my own; and I had a clear right to keep it; but it was no more my own than my vote is my own; and the threat of death to me, to extort my money, and the threat of destruction to the Union, to extort my vote, can scarcely be distinguished in principle.

A few words now to Republicans. *It is exceedingly desirable that all parts of this great Confederacy shall be at peace, and in harmony, one with another. Let us Republicans do our part to have it so. Even though much provoked, let us do nothing through passion and ill temper. Even though the southern people will not so much as listen to us, let us calmly consider their demands, and yield to them if, in our deliberate view of our duty, we possibly can.* Judging by all they say and do, and by the subject and nature of their controversy with us, let us determine, if we can, what will satisfy them.

Will they be satisfied if the Territories be unconditionally surrendered to them? We know they will not. In all their present complaints against us, the Territories are scarcely mentioned. Invasions and insurrections are the rage now. Will it satisfy them, if, in the future, we have nothing to do with invasions and insurrections? We know it will not. We so know, because we know we never had anything to do with invasions and insurrections; and yet this total abstaining does not exempt us from the charge and the denunciation.

The question recurs, what will satisfy them? Simply

this: We must not only let them alone, but we must some-how, convince them that we do let them alone. This, we know by experience, is no easy task. We have been so try-ing to convince them from the very beginning of our or-ganization, but with no success. In all our platforms and speeches we have constantly protested our purpose to let them alone; but this has had no tendency to convince them. Alike unavailing to convince them, is the fact that they have never detected a man of us in any attempt to disturb them.

These natural, and apparently adequate means all fail-ing, what will convince them? This, and this only: cease to call slavery *wrong*, and join them in calling it *right*. And this must be done thoroughly—done in *acts* as well as in *words*. Silence will not be tolerated—we must place our-selves avowedly with them. Senator Douglas's new sedi-tion law must be enacted and enforced, suppressing all declarations that slavery is wrong, whether made in poli-tics, in presses, in pulpits, or in private. We must arrest and return their fugitive slaves with greedy pleasure. We must pull down our Free-State Constitutions. The whole atmosphere must be disinfected from all taint of opposi-tion to slavery, before they will cease to believe that all their troubles proceed from us.

I am quite aware they do not state their case precisely in this way. Most of them would probably say to us, "Let us alone, do nothing to us, and say what you please about slavery." But we do let them alone—have never disturbed them—so that, after all, it is what we say, which dissatisfies them. They will continue to accuse us of doing, until we cease saying.

I am also aware they have not, as yet, in terms, demanded the overthrow of our Free-State Constitutions. Yet those Constitutions declare the wrong of slavery, with more solemn emphasis, than do all other sayings against it; and when all these others sayings shall have been silenced, the overthrow of these Constitutions will be demanded, and nothing be left to resist the demand. It is nothing to the contrary, that they do not demand the whole of this just now. Demanding what they do, and for the reason they do, they can voluntarily stop nowhere short of this consummation. Holding, as they do, that slavery is morally right, and socially elevating, they cannot cease to demand a full national recognition of it, as a legal right, and a social blessing.

Nor can we justifiably withhold this, on any ground save our conviction that slavery is wrong. If slavery is right, all words, acts, laws, and constitutions against it, are themselves wrong, and should be silenced, and swept away. If it is right, we cannot justly object to its nationality—its universality; if it is wrong, they cannot justly insist upon its extension—its enlargement. All they ask, we could readily grant, if we thought slavery right; all we ask, 70 they could as readily grant, if they thought it wrong.

Their thinking it right, and our thinking it wrong, is the precise fact upon which depends the whole controversy. Thinking it right, as they do, they are not to blame for desiring its full recognition, as being right; but, thinking it wrong, as we do, can we yield to them? Can we cast our votes with their view, and against our own? In view of our moral, social, and political responsibilities, can we do this?

Wrong as we think slavery is, we can yet afford to let it alone where it is, because that much is due to the necessity arising from its actual presence in the nation; but can we, while our votes will prevent it, allow it to spread into the National Territories, and to overrun us here in these Free States? If our sense of duty forbids this, then let us stand by our duty, fearlessly and effectively. Let us be diverted by none of those sophistical contrivances wherewith we are so industriously plied and belabored—contrivances such as groping for some middle ground between the right and the wrong, vain as the search for a man who should be neither a living man nor a dead man—such as a policy of "don't care" on a question about which all true men do care—such as Union appeals beseeching true Union men to yield to Disunionists, reversing the divine rule, and calling, not the sinners, but the righteous to repentance—such as invocations to Washington, imploring men to unsay what Washington said, and undo what Washington did.

Neither let us be slandered from our duty by false accusations against us, nor frightened from it by menaces of destruction to the Government nor of dungeons to ourselves. LET US HAVE FAITH THAT RIGHT MAKES MIGHT, AND IN THAT FAITH, LET US, TO THE END, DARE TO DO OUR DUTY AS WE UNDERSTAND IT.

Farewell Address at Springfield, Illinois:
February 11, 1861

My friends—

No one, not in my situation, can appreciate my feeling of sadness at this parting. To this place, and the kindness of these people, I owe everything. Here I have lived a quarter of a century, and have passed from a young to an old man. Here my children have been born, and one is buried. I now leave, not knowing when, or whether ever, I may return, with a task before me greater than that which rested upon Washington. Without the assistance of that Divine Being, who ever attended him, I cannot succeed. With that assistance I cannot fail. Trusting in Him, who can go with me, and remain with you and be everywhere for good, let us confidently hope that all will yet be well. To His care commending you, as I hope in your prayers you will commend me, I bid you an affectionate farewell.

Address in Independence Hall,
Philadelphia, Pennsylvania:
February 22, 1861

Mr. Cuyler:

I am filled with deep emotion at finding myself standing here in the place where were collected together the wisdom, the patriotism, the devotion to principle, from which sprang the institutions under which we live. You have kindly suggested to me that in my hands is the task of restoring peace to our distracted country. I can say in return, sir, that all the political sentiments I entertain have been drawn, so far as I have been able to draw them, from the sentiments which originated, and were given to the world from this hall in which we stand. I have never had a feeling politically that did not spring from the sentiments embodied in the Declaration of Independence. [Great cheering.] I have often pondered over the dangers which were incurred by the men who assembled here and adopted that Declaration of Independence—I have pondered over the toils that were endured by the officers and soldiers of the army, who achieved that independence. [Applause.] I have often inquired of myself, what great principle or idea it was that kept this confederacy so long

together. It was not the mere matter of the separation of

the colonies from the mother land; but something in that Declaration giving liberty, not alone to the people of this country, but hope to the world for all future time. [Great applause.] It was that which gave promise that in due time the weights should be lifted from the shoulders of all men, and that *all* should have an equal chance. [Cheers.] This is the sentiment embodied in that Declaration of Independence.

Now, my friends, can this country be saved upon that basis? If it can, I will consider myself one of the happiest men in the world if I can help to save it. If it can't be saved upon that principle, it will be truly awful. But, if this country cannot be saved without giving up that principle—I was about to say I would rather be assassinated on this spot than to surrender it. (Applause.)

Now, in my view of the present aspect of affairs, there is no need of bloodshed and war. There is no necessity for it. I am not in favor of such a course, and I may say in advance, there will be no bloodshed unless it be forced upon the government. The government will not use force unless force is used against it. [Prolonged applause and cries of "That's the proper sentiment."]

My friends, this is a wholly unprepared speech. I did not expect to be called upon to say a word when I came here—I supposed I was merely to do something towards 75 raising a flag. I may, therefore, have said something indiscreet, [cries of "no, no"], but I have said nothing but what I am willing to live by, and, in the pleasure of Almighty God, die by.

The Emancipation Proclamation:
January 1, 1863

BY THE PRESIDENT OF THE
UNITED STATES OF AMERICA:
A PROCLAMATION.

Whereas, on the twenty-second day of September, in the year of our Lord one thousand eight hundred and sixty-two, a proclamation was issued by the President of the United States, containing, among other things, the following, to wit:

"That on the first day of January, in the year of our Lord one thousand eight hundred and sixty-three, all persons held as slaves within any State or designated part of a State, the people whereof shall then be in rebellion against the United States, shall be then, thenceforward, and forever free; and the Executive Government of the United States, including the military and naval authority thereof, will recognize and maintain the freedom of such persons, and will do no act or acts to repress such persons, or any of them, in any efforts they may make for their actual freedom.

"That the Executive will, on the first day of January

aforesaid, by proclamation, designate the States and parts of States, if any, in which the people thereof, respectively, shall then be in rebellion against the United States; and the fact that any State, or the people thereof, shall on that day be, in good faith, represented in the Congress of the United States by members chosen thereto at elections wherein a majority of the qualified voters of such State shall have participated, shall, in the absence of strong countervailing testimony, be deemed conclusive evidence that such State, and the people thereof, are not then in rebellion against the United States."

Now, therefore I, Abraham Lincoln, President of the United States, by virtue of the power in me vested as Commander-in-Chief, of the Army and Navy of the United States in time of actual armed rebellion against authority and government of the United States, and as a fit and necessary war measure for suppressing said rebellion, do, on this first day of January, in the year of our Lord one thousand eight hundred and sixty-three, and in accordance with my purpose so to do publicly proclaimed for the full period of one hundred days, from the day first above mentioned, order and designate as the States and parts of States wherein the people thereof respectively, are this day in rebellion against the United States, the following, to wit:

Arkansas, Texas, Louisiana, (except the Parishes of St. 78 Bernard, Plaquemines, Jefferson, St. Johns, St. Charles,

St. James, Ascension, Assumption, Terrebonne, Lafourche, St. Mary, St. Martin, and Orleans, including the City of New Orleans) Mississippi, Alabama, Florida, Georgia, South Carolina, North Carolina, and Virginia, (except the forty-eight counties designated as West Virginia, and also the counties of Berkley, Accomac, Northampton, Elizabeth City, York, Princess Ann, and Norfolk, including the cities of Norfolk & Portsmouth); and which excepted parts are, for the present, left precisely as if this proclamation were not issued.

And by virtue of the power, and for the purpose aforesaid, I do order and declare that all persons held as slaves within said designated States, and parts of States, are, and henceforward shall be free; and that the executive government of the United States, including the military and naval authorities thereof, will recognize and maintain the freedom of said persons.

And I hereby enjoin upon the people so declared to be free to abstain from all violence, unless in necessary self-defence; and I recommend to them that, in all cases when allowed, they labor faithfully for reasonable wages.

And I further declare and make known, that such persons of suitable condition, will be received into the armed service of the United States to garrison forts, positions, stations, and other places, and to man vessels of all sorts in said service.

And upon this act, sincerely believed to be an act of

justice, warranted by the Constitution, upon military necessity, I invoke the considerate judgment of mankind, and the gracious favor of Almighty God.

In witness whereof, I have hereunto set my hand and caused the seal of the United States to be affixed.

[L.S.] Done at the City of Washington, this first day of January, in the year of our Lord one thousand eight hundred and sixty-three, and of the Independence of the United States of America the eighty-seventh.

By the President:

Abraham Lincoln

WILLIAM H. SEWARD, Secretary of State.

Address at the Dedication of the Cemetery at Gettysburg, Pennsylvania: November 19, 1863

Four score and seven years ago our fathers brought forth on this continent, a new nation, conceived in liberty, and dedicated to the proposition that all men are created equal.

Now we are engaged in a great civil war, testing whether that nation, or any nation so conceived and so dedicated, can long endure. We are met on a great battlefield of that war. We have come to dedicate a portion of that field, as a final resting place for those who here gave their lives that that nation might live. It is altogether fitting and proper that we should do this.

But, in a larger sense, we cannot dedicate—we cannot consecrate—we cannot hallow—this ground. The brave men, living and dead, who struggled here, have consecrated it, far above our poor power to add or detract. The world will little note, nor long remember what we say here, but it can never forget what they did here. It is for us the living, rather, to be dedicated here to the unfinished work which they who fought here have thus far so nobly advanced. It is rather for us to be here dedicated to the great task remaining before us—that from these hon- 81

ored dead we take increased devotion to that cause for which they gave the last full measure of devotion—that we here highly resolve that these dead shall not have died in vain—that this nation, under God, shall have a new birth of freedom—and that government of the people, by the people, for the people, shall not perish from the earth.

Address to the 166th Ohio Regiment:
August 22, 1864

I suppose you are going home to see your families and friends. For the service you have done in this great struggle in which we are engaged I present you sincere thanks for myself and the country. I almost always feel inclined, when I happen to say anything to soldiers, to impress upon them in a few brief remarks the importance of success in this contest. It is not merely for today, but for all time to come that we should perpetuate for our children's children this great and free government, which we have enjoyed all our lives. I beg you to remember this, not merely for my sake, but for yours. I happen temporarily to occupy this big White House. I am a living witness that any one of your children may look to come here as my father's child has. It is in order that each of you may have through this free government which we have enjoyed, an open field and a fair chance for your industry, enterprise and intelligence; that you may all have equal privileges in the race of life, with all its desirable human aspirations. It is for this the struggle should be maintained, that we may not lose our birthright—not only for one, but for two or three years. The nation is worth fighting for, to secure such an inestimable jewel.

Second Inaugural Address, Washington, D.C.:
March 4, 1865

Fellow-Countrymen:

At this second appearing to take the oath of the presidential office, there is less occasion for an extended address than there was at the first. Then a statement, somewhat in detail, of a course to be pursued, seemed fitting and proper. Now, at the expiration of four years, during which public declarations have been constantly called forth on every point and phase of the great contest which still absorbs the attention, and engrosses the energies of the nation, little that is new could be presented. The progress of our arms, upon which all else chiefly depends, is as well known to the public as to myself; and it is, I trust, reasonably satisfactory and encouraging to all. With high hope for the future, no prediction in regard to it is ventured.

On the occasion corresponding to this four years ago, all thoughts were anxiously directed to an impending civil war. All dreaded it—all sought to avert it. While the inaugural address was being delivered from this place, devoted altogether to *saving* the Union without war, insurgent agents were in the city seeking to *destroy* it without war—seeking to dissolve the Union, and divide effects, by negotiation. Both parties deprecated war; but one of them would *make* war rather than let the nation survive; and the other would *accept* war rather than let it perish. And the war came.

One eighth of the whole population were colored slaves, not distributed generally over the Union, but localized in the southern part of it. These slaves constituted a peculiar and powerful interest. All knew that this interest was, somehow, the cause of the war. To strengthen, perpetuate, and extend this interest was the object for which the insurgents would rend the Union, even by war; while the government claimed no right to do more than to restrict the territorial enlargement of it. Neither party expected for the war, the magnitude, or the duration, which it has already attained. Neither anticipated that the *cause* of the conflict might cease with, or even before, the conflict itself should cease. Each looked for an easier triumph, and a result less fundamental and astounding. Both read the same Bible, and pray to the same God; and each invokes His aid against the other. It may seem strange that any men should dare to ask a just God's assistance in wringing their bread from the sweat of other men's faces; but let us judge not that we be not judged. The prayers of both could not be answered; that of neither has been answered fully. The Almighty has His own purposes. "Woe unto the world because of offences! for it must needs be that offences come; but woe to that man by whom the offence cometh!" If we shall suppose that American slavery is one of those offences which, in the providence of God, must needs come, but which, having continued through His appointed time, He now wills to remove, and that He gives to both North and South, this terrible war, as the woe due to those by whom the offence came, shall we discern therein any departure from those divine attributes which the believers in a Living God always ascribe to Him? Fondly do we hope—fervently do we pray—that this mighty scourge of war may speedily pass away. Yet, if God wills that it continue, until all the wealth piled by the bondman's two hundred and fifty years of unrequited toil shall be sunk, and until every drop of blood drawn with the lash, shall be paid by another drawn with the sword, as was said three thousand years ago, so still it must be said "the judgments of the Lord, are true and righteous altogether."

With malice toward none; with charity for all; with firmness in the right, as God gives us to see the right, let us strive on to finish the work we are in; to bind up the nation's wounds; to care for him who shall have borne the battle, and for his widow, and his orphan—to do all which may achieve and cherish a just, and a lasting peace, among ourselves, and with all nations.

LOUISA MAY ALCOTT · *An Old-Fashioned Thanksgiving and Other Stories*

HANS CHRISTIAN ANDERSEN · *The Emperor's New Clothes*

J. M. BARRIE · *Peter Pan in Kensington Gardens*

WILLIAM BLAKE · *Songs of Innocence and Experience*

GEOFFREY CHAUCER · *The Wife of Bath and Other Canterbury Tales*

ANTON CHEKHOV · *The Black Monk and Peasants*

SAMUEL TAYLOR COLERIDGE · *The Rime of the Ancient Mariner*

COLETTE · *Gigi*

JOSEPH CONRAD · *Youth*

ROALD DAHL · *Lamb to the Slaughter and Other Stories*

ROBERTSON DAVIES · *A Gathering of Ghost Stories*

FYODOR DOSTOYEVSKY · *The Grand Inquisitor*

SIR ARTHUR CONAN DOYLE · *The Man with the Twisted Lip*
   and *The Adventure of the Devil's Foot*

RALPH WALDO EMERSON · *Nature*

OMER ENGLEBERT (TRANS.) · *The Lives of the Saints*

FANNIE FARMER · *The Original 1896 Boston Cooking-School Cook Book*

EDWARD FITZGERALD (TRANS.) · *The Rubáiyát of Omar Khayyám*

ROBERT FROST · *The Road Not Taken and Other Early Poems*

GABRIEL GARCÍA MÁRQUEZ · *Bon Voyage, Mr President and Other Stories*

NIKOLAI GOGOL · *The Overcoat and The Nose*

GRAHAM GREENE · *Under the Garden*

JACOB AND WILHELM GRIMM · *Grimm's Fairy Tales*

NATHANIEL HAWTHORNE · *Young Goodman Brown and Other Stories*

O. HENRY · *The Gift of the Magi and Other Stories*

WASHINGTON IRVING · *Rip Van Winkle and The Legend of Sleepy Hollow*

HENRY JAMES · *Daisy Miller*

V. S. VERNON JONES (TRANS.) · *Aesop's Fables*

JAMES JOYCE · *The Dead*

GARRISON KEILLOR · *Truckstop and Other Lake Wobegon Stories*

FOR THE BEST IN PAPERBACKS, LOOK FOR THE

In every corner of the world, on every subject under the sun, Penguin represents quality and variety—the very best in publishing today.

For complete information about books available from Penguin—including Puffins, Penguin Classics, and Arkana—and how to order them, write to us at the appropriate address below. Please note that for copyright reasons the selection of books varies from country to country.

In the United States: Please write to *Consumer Sales, Penguin USA, P.O. Box 999, Dept. 17109, Bergenfield, New Jersey 07621-0120.* VISA and MasterCard holders call 1-800-253-6476 to order all Penguin titles.

In Canada: Please write to *Penguin Books Canada Ltd, 10 Alcorn Avenue, Suite 300, Toronto, Ontario M4V 3B2.*

In the United Kingdom: Please write to *Dept. JC, Penguin Books Ltd, FREEPOST, West Drayton, Middlesex UB7 0BR.*